The Sand Dragon

With thanks to Alex and Edward

First published 2005
Evans Brothers Limited
2A Portman Mansions
Chiltern Street
London W1U 6NR

British Library Cataloguing in Publication Data
Swallow, Su
        Sand Dragon. – (Twisters)
        1. Children's stories – Pictorial works
        I. Title
        823.9'14 [J]

ISBN 0237529424
13-digit ISBN (from 1 January 2007) 9780237529420

Printed in China by WKT Company Limited

Series Editor: Nick Turpin
Design: Robert Walster
Production: Jenny Mulvanny
Series Consultant: Gill Matthews

The Sand Dragon

Su Swallow
and Silvia Raga

The seaside!

5

Splish splash!

6

Look!

Hurray!

12

"What's that?" said Mum.

13

"A sand dragon."
They both went home.

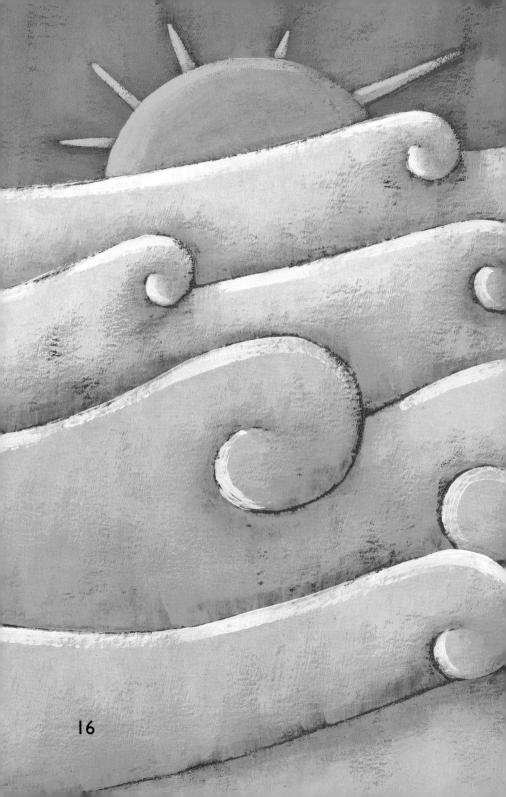

16

The waves splashed,

17

the dragon swam,

19

and nibbled,

21

and danced.

The waves moved back.

The dragon lay on the
sand to dry.

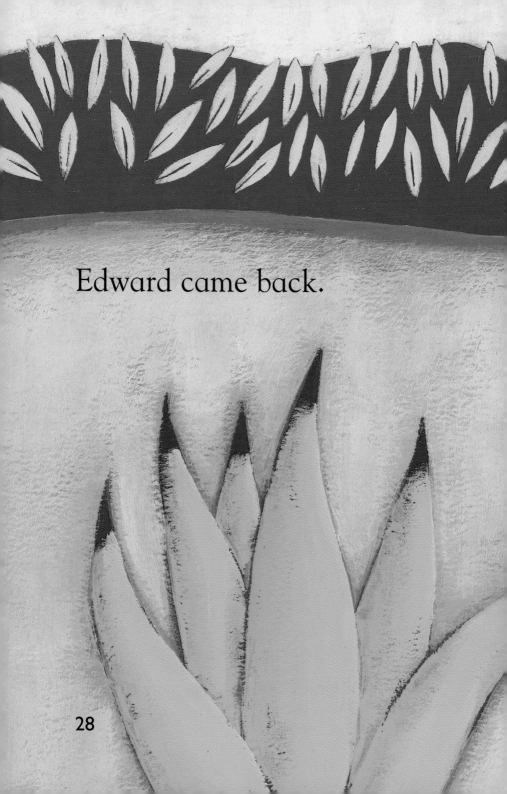

Edward came back.

"Mummy, my sand dragon
hasn't moved all night!"

31

Why not try reading another Twisters book?

Not-so-silly Sausage by Stella Gurney and Liz Million
ISBN 0 237 52875 4

Nick's Birthday by Jane Oliver and Silvia Raga
ISBN 0 237 52896 7

Out Went Sam by Nick Turpin and Barbara Nascimbeni
ISBN 0 237 52894 0

Yummy Scrummy by Paul Harrison and Belinda Worsley
ISBN 0 237 52876 2

Squelch! by Kay Woodward and Stefania Colnaghi
ISBN 0 237 52895 9

Sally Sails the Seas by Stella Gurney and Belinda Worsley
ISBN 0 237 52893 2

Billy on the Ball by Paul Harrison and Silvia Raga
ISBN 0 237 52926 2

Countdown by Kay Woodward and Ofra Amit
ISBN 0 237 52927 0

One Wet Welly by Gill Matthews and Belinda Worsley
ISBN 0 237 52928 9

Sand Dragon by Su Swallow and Silvia Raga
ISBN 0 237 52929 7

Cave-baby and the Mammoth by Vivian French and Lisa Williams
ISBN 0 237 52931 9

Albert Liked Ladders by Su Swallow and Barbara Nascimbeni
ISBN 0 237 52930 0